SOCCER STARS

NEYMAR

SARAH MACHAJEWSKI

PowerKiDS
press™

New York

Published in 2019 by The Rosen Publishing Group, Inc.
29 East 21st Street, New York, NY 10010

First Edition

Editor: Elizabeth Krajnik
Book Design: Michael Flynn

Photo Credits: Cover (Neymar), p. 1 Rob Newell - CameraSport/CameraSport/Getty Images; cover (stadium background) winui/Shutterstock.com; cover (player glow) Nejron Photo/Shutterstock.com; pp. 3, 23, 24 (background) Narong Jongsirikul/ Shutterstock.com; pp. 4, 6, 8–10, 12, 14, 16–18, 20, 22 (ball background) DRN Studio/Shutterstock.com; p. 5 Aurelien Meunier/Getty Images Sport/Getty Images; p. 6 Manuel Queimadelos Alonso/Getty Images Sport/Getty Images; p. 7 https://en.wikipedia.org/wiki/Neymar#/media/File:Neymar_PSG.jpg; p. 8 Victor Moriyama/Getty Images News/Getty Images; p. 9 Mark Herreid/Shutterstock. com; p. 10 Chekyravaa/Shutterstock.com; p. 11 Matthew Ashton - AMA/Getty Images Sport/Getty Images; p. 13 Laurence Griffiths/Getty Images Sport/Getty Images; p. 15 MAURICIO LIMA/AFP/Getty Images; p. 16 Stuart Franklin - FIFA/ FIFA/Getty Images; p. 17 vipcomm/Shutterstock.com; p. 19 DANIEL GARCIA/AFP/ Getty Images; p. 21 Guillaume Ruoppolo/Icon Sport/Getty Images; p. 22 Jefferson Bernardes/Shutterstock.com.

Cataloging-in-Publication Data

Names: Machajewski, Sarah.
Title: Neymar / Sarah Machajewski.
Description: New York : PowerKids Press, 2019. | Series: Soccer stars | Includes glossary and index.
Identifiers: ISBN 9781538345122 (pbk.) | ISBN 9781538343531 (library bound) | ISBN 9781538345139 (6 pack)
Subjects: LCSH: Neymar, 1992–Juvenile literature. | Soccer players–Brazil–Biography- -Juvenile literature.
Classification: LCC GV942.7.P42 M33 2019 | DDC 796.334092 B–dc23

Manufactured in the United States of America

CPSIA Compliance Information: Batch #CWPK19 For Further Information contact Rosen Publishing, New York, New York at 1-800-237-9932

CONTENTS

RISING STAR

Neymar! Neymar! Neymar! If you attended a soccer match in Paris, France, you would probably hear people shouting this throughout the stadium. That's because when soccer star Neymar da Silva Santos Junior takes to the field, he's unstoppable!

Neymar, as he's commonly known, is one of soccer's most **prominent** stars. He's attracted attention from fans and teams all over the world because he's a leading goalscorer and can play with both feet! Neymar's abilities have taken the world of soccer by storm. He's on his way to becoming one of the greatest players in the history of the sport!

STAR POWER

Many athletes get involved in their sport at an early age, but that doesn't mean they stop working hard once they've become successful. Neymar has said, "I'm always trying to perfect everything—dribbling, shooting, headers, and control. You can always improve."

NEYMAR'S STYLE OF PLAY HAS MADE HIM A SOCCER STAR. HE IS KNOWN FOR HIS DRIBBLING SKILLS, TRICKS, AND PLAYMAKING ABILITY.

SOCCER IN HIS GENES

Neymar was born on February 5, 1992, in Mogi das Cruzes, a neighborhood in São Paolo, Brazil. Neymar's name is known throughout the world of soccer, but he isn't the first in his family to play. Neymar's father was a **professional** soccer player, too.

Neymar Sr.'s **career** ended when his son was just a few years old. He worked many jobs to support his family, including working as a mechanic, a bricklayer, and for the city. Neymar's mother worked as a cook. Today, Neymar's family is very supportive. His dad is his **agent**.

NEYMAR SR.

NEYMAR SR. HAS SAID HE WASN'T A GREAT SOCCER PLAYER. HIS SON, ON THE OTHER HAND, IS ONE OF THE GREATS!

STARTING YOUNG

Soccer is one of the world's most popular sports, and it's especially popular in Brazil. Neymar began playing soccer when he was a young boy, and he was a **natural** from the beginning.

Like other children in Brazil, playing soccer with friends was one of Neymar's hobbies. Neymar grew up playing soccer on the streets of Brazil. He also played **futsal**. He was good at it all.

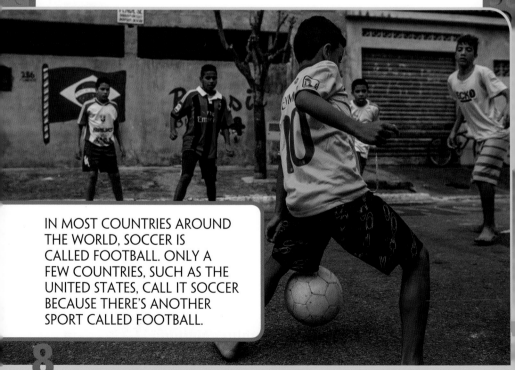

IN MOST COUNTRIES AROUND THE WORLD, SOCCER IS CALLED FOOTBALL. ONLY A FEW COUNTRIES, SUCH AS THE UNITED STATES, CALL IT SOCCER BECAUSE THERE'S ANOTHER SPORT CALLED FOOTBALL.

When he was just five or six years old, he wanted to play against older boys in his town—even though they were a lot bigger than him!

A TRUE TALENT

A true sports talent doesn't need the most expensive gear to master the sport. A talented athlete will be good no matter where he or she is playing, or what kind of equipment they're using. Just ask Neymar! He learned the sport from street football, where sandals were used for the goal posts and sometimes, a rock was the soccer ball. It didn't matter to Neymar, though. "I just wanted to play," he has said.

And he did. Neymar joined Portuguesa Santista's youth team and, when his family moved to São Vicente in 2003, he joined Santos FC.

TODAY, MANY PEOPLE AROUND THE WORLD KNOW NEYMAR'S NAME. THEY EVEN WEAR HIS JERSEY AND CHEER HIM ON!

ONE-OF-A-KIND STYLE

Neymar's **passion** for his sport helped him stand out. So did his ball-handling skills. Whether he's juggling the ball, rolling it, cradling it, or kicking it over his head, Neymar's style is—and always has been—one of a kind.

Teams throughout Brazil soon began noticing Neymar. At 11 years old, Santos FC **recruited** him to play on the youth team and attend the youth academy. Word of Neymar's talent began to spread, and European teams tried to recruit him. However, Santos paid to keep him in Brazil. Neymar was young, but he was a player in high demand.

STAR POWER

When Neymar was 14 years old, he had a trial with Real Madrid, a professional soccer club in Spain. Real Madrid's interest in Neymar is why Santos had to pay so much to keep him.

NEYMAR PLAYS THE POSITION OF FORWARD. FORWARDS SCORE GOALS FOR THEIR TEAM.

INSTANT SUCCESS

Neymar played for Santos's youth teams from 2003 to 2009. During that time, he became a great player. In 2009, he made his debut, or first official appearance, with Santos's first team, which is the club's most **senior** team. He was just 17 years old, but he was a near-instant success.

In a game against Oeste, Neymar played for just 30 minutes. That's all it took for him to live up to the **hype** surrounding him. He was fast, skilled, and confident. These qualities have become part of Neymar's trademark style. When he takes to the field, the fans get cheering—especially when he scores a goal.

STAR POWER

While playing with Santos, Neymar won a lot of awards. Among them, he won the South American Footballer of the Year title in 2011 and 2012.

NEYMAR'S FIRST SEASON WAS A SUCCESS. HE SCORED 14 GOALS AND HELPED HIS TEAM GET TO THE FINAL ROUND OF THE 2009 CAMPEONATO PAULISTA.

A HOUSEHOLD NAME

Neymar's second season with Santos was even better than his first. The 2010 season really put him on the map, making him a household name among soccer fans.

That year, Santos won the Copa do Brasil in large part thanks to Neymar. He scored five goals in an 8–1 **victory**. After leading his team to the country's top soccer title, Neymar was officially a star.

2011 FIFA PUSKÁS AWARD

Even though Neymar was now famous, some people doubted his abilities, saying he was too scrawny, or thin. Neymar never let this **criticism** hold him back, and he continued to be a strong player.

STAR POWER

In 2011, Neymar helped Santos win their first Copa Libertadores title since 1963. That year, Neymar won the FIFA Puskás Award.

100TH GOAL

Neymar's star power only increased during the 2011–2012 and 2012–2013 seasons. He had more assists and goals than ever before. On February 5, 2012, Neymar scored his 100th professional goal during a match against Palmeiras in the Campeonato Paulista. He was just 20 years old.

In June 2013, Neymar signed a five-year **contract** with FC Barcelona, or Barça, a Spanish professional club. He joined the ranks with soccer superstars Lionel Messi and Luis Suárez.

Before Neymar left for Spain, he helped Brazil succeed in the 2013 FIFA Confederations Cup. He won the Golden Ball award for being the best player of the tournament.

NEYMAR PLAYED FOR THE BRAZILIAN NATIONAL TEAM DURING THE 2012 FIFA WORLD CUP IN JAPAN AND THE 2012 SUMMER OLYMPICS IN LONDON, ENGLAND.

NEYMAR GETS HURT

Neymar entered La Liga with a bang. His quick footwork and overall talent helped him score 39 goals in the 2014–2015 season. That season, Barça won many titles, including the La Liga title, the Copa del Rey, and the UEFA Champions League. Neymar was named the La Liga Best World Player and named to the UEFA Champions League Squad of the Season during the 2014–2015 season.

Even though Neymar has been very successful, it hasn't always been easy. In 2014, he suffered a back injury during the 2014 FIFA World Cup. It was a life-changing event for Neymar, his team, and his fans.

STAR POWER

On August 3, 2017, Neymar was released from Barcelona to join the French professional club Paris Saint-Germain as a forward. He made his debut with the team on August 13, 2017.

AS A TOP ATHLETE, NEYMAR HAS TO STAY HEALTHY AND IN GOOD SHAPE. SERIOUS INJURIES CAN END AN ATHLETE'S CAREER.

ONE OF THE GREATS

Luckily, Neymar recovered from his back injury and soon returned to playing soccer. And he did it with his trademark Neymar **flair**. In 2016, Neymar led his country to victory on their own soil during the 2016 Summer Olympics in Rio de Janeiro, Brazil. As captain of the Brazilian national team, Neymar scored the winning goal during a shootout with Germany. Fans all over the world—and especially in Brazil—went wild!

Whether lighting up the field in his home country or scoring goals all over Europe, Neymar is a true soccer star. Could he be one of the greatest players ever? He's certainly on his way!

GLOSSARY

agent: A person who acts or does business for another person.

career: A period of time spent doing a job or activity.

contract: A legal agreement between people, companies, and other groups.

criticism: The act of finding fault.

flair: An unusual and appealing quality or style.

futsal: A sport similar to soccer and played with five-person teams on a basketball court with no walls and a smaller, low-bouncing ball.

hype: Publicity, or attention that is given to someone or something by the media.

natural: Someone who is good at doing something from the first time it is done.

passion: A strong feeling or emotion.

professional: Taking part in a sport to make money.

prominent: Important and well-known or easily noticed or seen.

recruit: To find suitable people and get them to join a company, an organization, or a team.

senior: Higher in standing or rank than another person or team in the same position.

victory: The act of defeating an enemy or opponent.

INDEX

WEBSITES

Due to the changing nature of Internet links, PowerKids Press has developed an online list of websites related to the subject of this book. This site is updated regularly. Please use this link to access the list: www.powerkidslinks.com/socstars/neymar